T0208587

BARCELONA COFFEE

ADULT STORIES

CRISTINA ROLDÁN

BALBOA.
PRESS

A DIVISION OF HAY HOUSE

Balboa Press books may be ordered through booksellers or by contacting:

Balboa Press
A Division of Hay House
1663 Liberty Drive
Bloomington, IN 47403
www.balboapress.com
1 (877) 407-4847

Because of the dynamic nature of the Internet, any web addresses or
links contained in this book may have changed since publication and
may no longer be valid. The views expressed in this work are solely those
of the author and do not necessarily reflect the views of the publisher,
and the publisher hereby disclaims any responsibility for them.

This is a work of fiction. Names, characters, businesses, places, events
and incidents are either the products of the author's imagination
or used in a fictitious manner. Any resemblance to actual persons,
living or dead, or actual events is purely coincidental.

Interior Image Credit: Cristina Roldán
Cover Image Credit: Cristina Roldán/Mariah Rodriguez

Print information available on the last page.

ISBN: 978-1-9822-3581-9 (sc)
ISBN: 978-1-9822-3583-3 (hc)
ISBN: 978-1-9822-3582-6 (e)

Library of Congress Control Number: 2019915269

Balboa Press rev. date: 10/16/2019

I adjusted the belt while the voice of the stewardess said the usual. We are already flying. Pep, at my side, is calmly drinking some fruit juice. The trip was going to be long and boring. "We will have some fun while the lights are out", Pep tells me with a wink. His son, Pep Junior, is sitting some seats further back near a chunky redhead who, from the beginning, before going through Customs, had smiled at him provocatively. "That chick is nice", he commented to his father and me. "Well, so you are going to be distracted." He is fourteen years old and is very nervous. The redhead is twice his age: her name is Meritchell and works in Barcelona's city hall. We live in the city and have just left it, enthusiastic about "helping" the guerrillas in El Salvador.

We are not alone; there are about fifteen of us. The only one I know is Jordi — a friend of Pep — and Giorgio, an Italian from Milan who was convinced to join our cause by Pep, who belongs to the Communist

Party. Last night, while we were stargazing from the cute penthouse Pep has in L'Hospitalet, a quiet working-class neighbourhood in Barcelona, he told me how important it is that we collaborate to help these poor people. I totally agree with him, although I have my doubts about the effectiveness of assistance that consists of spending a few days of a holiday by their side, because we cannot afford to leave our jobs for more time. The moon lit up a large pretty smokestack in the middle of the square where Pep lives, giving it a magical look. We hugged and went inside to finish getting ready for the trip. Meritchell walked by us towards the toilet and says: "Amparo Soria is with us". "Who is Amparo Soria?" Pep asks. "You know her; she is one of the actresses from the Bagdad, the nightclub near Las Ramblas, the one that does the big erotic number, with the two black guys and the Pekingese dog." "Oh, yeah; I remember perfectly. The girl was so lively! What is she going to do in El Salvador?" "She will most likely be getting off on the previous layover", yawned Pep, who was nodding off as we talked.

I fell asleep right away, too. I was beat, extremely tired. I woke up when the plane landed at the airport in Mexico. All I am carrying is my backpack and this has saved me from problems with luggage. We got ready to wait for the connecting flight to Tuxtla, the capital of the state of Oaxaca. It arrived on time and when we went to find our places, we discovered that Amparo Soria, "the actress from the Bagdad", was also coming with the group. Pep Junior was very pumped up about Meritchell. The plane was very old and I fell asleep in Pep's arms. I woke up when we were arriving in Tapachula. The plane stopped and we landed on a kind of potato plantation and disembarked. The heat was pressing and dense, hot air that enters your lungs and leaves you with a kind of apathy and reluctance to move, with every motion measured. Alain was waiting for us with a kind of jeep that had seen better days; we had to cross through Guatemala. What an idea of the expedition's organiser to have us go to Mexico! All I could think about was a good shower, about letting the water run and wake me up from the trip which, before it had even started, was already becoming a drag to get through. But who could have convinced me to travel these byways?

"What a drag!" "So now the lady is complaining", says Pep, but I convince Alain to stop in a tiny hamlet opposite a cottage where, from the door, one can see a little curtain made from a kind of crochet traditional to the region and an advertisement for a local beverage. The place is filthy; there is no toilet or river or mineral water for washing, which causes me to take some of the local beverage to use for washing up a little. The Indian — who actually looks more Chinese — hands it to me with a smile. I try it the best I can in a kind of toilet I improvised for cleaning my butt. "Good God! It is pure alcohol and sticky, too." I am angry enough that I do not want anyone to know how ticked off I am, so I return to the group with a smile. The Indian woman brought us some corn tortillas with some kind of spicy hot vegetables and the beverage that I had just tried out below. Above, it also tastes repulsive. The stupid bitch smiles when she sees me and then brings me an ice-cold Coke that leads me to make up with her. We are close to Tapachula on the Pacific, and Alain explains to us that we are about to enter virgin forest. We will enter Guatemala through a very special border checkpoint. But I had barely woken up from my deep sleep in the jeep. Pep has my passport and I carry my backpack full of panties or briefs so that I have enough of them and can change them twice a day for as long as the trip lasts. We pass through Quetzaltenango, Totonicapan, Chiquimula; we will enter El Salvador via Cojutepeque. We were told that the guerrillas on both sides are some tough bastards, so it is important to be careful.

Between its being very old and way overloaded, you could say the jeep was a kind of cocktail shaker. I complain about the road. Suddenly, I open my eyes because Alain stops at a checkpoint. He has some kind of special "permission pass" about which I know little and care even less. Then I realise we are passing through pure jungle and that I quite like it. I ask them to stop for a moment to take a photo as a souvenir. But especially Amparo — now being caressed by Pep Junior (the kid definitely does not quit; what a holiday he is going to have) — well, it could be said that Amparo was in a hurry to get there. Pep has been divorced for two years and lives with his son. We were together during the last Easter holiday in Holland with the bikes and the three of us get along fine. My daughter is currently with her father for the summer months and I am here, worried about the period that I am not getting. In the jeep, they are discussing Rafael's ideals; he leads the patrol we are going to visit. The guy has some balls. Jordi also works at Caixa de Girona with Pep and they have known each other for some time as Party members. I realise we are in a hurry to reach point X because the helicopter coming from Cuba with weapons and medicine has to land.

The jeep passes through forgotten, desolate, hamlets. You can feel the poverty that reigns supreme in them. The children touch my heart; I would take them all away with me. Farming is a bit neglected; there are some cornfields near the town, but that is all. In Guatemala and El Salvador, the staple food is corn tortillas and — with luck — they are eaten with beans and rice. The hunger and chaos caused by the war are palpable.

Night falls like a fast-flying raven's wing when we return to El Salvador over a winding road that makes us get out and walk, for the jeep can no longer continue. We arrived in the camp quite late in the evening. Rafael Mendez was waiting for us. Alain showed that he knew the road well. There are some fifty people at the camp. There is one guy who is smoking pot as Amparo says; her conversation and language are about as polished as her show in Barcelona. Rafael accompanies us to our tents and, while preparing a kind of jug, that here they call her "chuca". I go out to shower under a little waterfall just ten metres from our tent. That is when I became aware of how high we are. You could say that it is possible to reach the moon and that I can grab it with my hand. It is a full moon and is shining in all its splendour.

I finish my shower and walk naked over the rocks because I have no towel. I reach upward to try and catch a moonbeam, something I love, and I see a shadow. It is Giorgio, from Milan, who lends me his shirt so I can dry myself. This does not take long, because the weather is searingly hot, even at night. I sit down on a rock and talk with him while he smokes a cigarette. I look for my bathing suits, which left around there, for I had a strong desire to shower and rid myself of all the dirt from that viscous and sticky drink clinging to my legs. When I come back to where Giorgio is, he is already on his third cigarette. "Look at those beautiful stars. They look close enough to touch." "Look, this one is Delphinus, and this other one, Columba, and this other one is Betel Hauser, a name that I love", I say. "Oh, here you are, little one," said Pep, who is coming. I am a year older than him but — by reflex or whatever — he has a paternalistic attitude towards me. "Yes, dear. I have just showered. Giorgio lent me his shirt so I could dry myself", I tell him while I change behind a bush. I brought new red panties; red brings me good luck. I push him towards the shower (because if not, he will have to wait for me to visit him in his sleeping bag tonight) and I continue chatting with Giorgio. It appears that he also travels because he loves visiting countries. A guitar sounds and the atmosphere is rather romantic. The Italian has been working in Rome since a year ago for an American company, a multinational that manufactures various products. He has been able to maintain his relationship with Pep as his parents live in Barcelona and he goes there to visit them quite frequently.

We laugh at ourselves and the quixotic nature of the trip, since it cost me an arm and a leg (which I certainly cannot afford to lose). Pep has had to help me out with a small loan that I will pay back little by little. Meritchell and Pep Junior arrived. They settled in and brought us some very good American canned goods; even Pep had to admit it. Tomorrow they are going to work and I will take the opportunity to visit the camp and take some notes because I assume — judging by what little I saw when I arrived — the place is very beautiful in a green jungle style, but not in the least bit practical. Based on what we talked about with Rafael, we are right at the X mark. The helicopter will land tomorrow in the early morning. Pep and I say goodbye to the group and go to the tent. I turn on the torch that I brought in my backpack and Pep hugs me, naked. When we are about to get into my sleeping bag, I see some tiny pimples on his penis, right at the tip. "I am not going to bed with you, kid." "They must be from the ones from Bilbao I met in Cuba last year, one of them had blennorrhoea. Damn those bitches from Bilbao; they have ruined my holiday! People should demand a health certification card before going to bed with someone." "I told you,

Pep. I am getting into my sleeping bag alone and I am going to sleep right away."

When I wake up, Pep is no longer in his sleeping bag. I look at my watch, but it had stopped at two; maybe it was the altitude. I stretch, get out of my sleeping bag and head to the waterfall to shower. It is as if the water comes out lukewarm. "It is so nice." Without drying off, I put on my t-shirt and the new panties and squeeze into my jeans. When I am putting on my trainers, I hear a conversation in Italian, not far from the rock where I am sitting. As I am curious by nature, I quickly finish putting on my shoes and step behind a tree, in an attempt to find out who it is and what is being said, because I learned Italian during the year I lived in Rome when I was studying painting. It is Giorgio and a man around seventy-five, thin, scrawny, rather tall, and his remaining hair is thin, white and wispy. He has tortoiseshell glasses, is deeply suntanned and his extremely long face is deeply furrowed with wrinkles. Elegantly dressed in white, his trousers are held up by matching braces. He is handing Giorgio a medium-sized cardboard of the kind used to store Christmas tree decorations. Giorgio speaks very softly. "Thank you, Professor Sigal." Indeed, Herr Professor has a strong accent and must have been in a hurry, for he speaks hurriedly and I can barely understand what he is saying. "Remember, Giorgio, just a few drops in the drink and the plan will be perfect." "Remember, due to its high HTLV-II content, it cannot be exposed to light before being inoculated into the drink, and now I must leave. I still have a long way to go before I reach the plateau where the plane is waiting for me." I return to the tent because Pep might become worried. Meanwhile, I see Amparo Soria, who is approaching me; she has not seen me and heads over to Giorgio. The two melt into a passionate embrace. There is no sign of Pep in the tent. I look in my backpack for my little pocket encyclopaedia and search for HTLV Type 2 virus. Horrifying! It is the formula of the AIDS virus.

I am most definitely going to suffer from thirst on

this trip. I return to the waterfall and gulp down large amounts of water. The scenery is magnificent, different clouds, with green predominating from the really lush vegetation exploding everywhere. The sky is indigo blue and the sun has been beating down fiercely for some time now. I look at it and it hurts me. It is like one of those ripe oranges exported from Spain for sale in foreign markets.

As I head to the camp, which is a little further away, my mind is bubbling with several ideas to prevent Giorgio from contaminating the water with the AIDS virus. I do not know who is on what side and it is going to be hard. And there is also Amparo, who is his accomplice. What an ingenious way of destroying an entire regiment without arousing suspicion in the national press and I myself even spoke to Giorgio yesterday about our quixotic adventure. What a fool I am! My mother is always telling me, "You do not wise up; everyone is going to mess with you, even the dumbest ones". And maybe she is right.

Before reaching the camp, I run my fingers through my hair, looking at myself in a small mirror I always carry in my jeans, and make my entrance to the camp as gleamingly as I can. There, among others, I see Captain Mendez drinking some kind of yerba mate and talking with Pep, who was smoking a Cohiba. "My God! Will you — a man's man, with that huge body — get sick from the AIDS virus? And, my dear homebody Pep, blennorrhoea can happen, but I do not want to imagine you with that terrible disease." "Hello, little one. How did you sleep?" "Like a baby, dear." "Come and have a kind of yerba mate they make around here." I sit down close to them and peel a banana. Today must be a bank holiday because I do not hear a single shot. Alain sits down with us and I find out that the helicopter has already landed with weapons and medicines sent from Cuba. There are some strange cartridges containing chemical weapons capable of transforming the most beautiful human into a horrible post-galactic beast in less time than it takes a rooster to crow. A shudder runs down my back. I —who was breathing deeply in the belief I was in the middle of a green space, in the middle of such an unpolluted prophylactic forest — have an explosive sitting under my buttocks — my arse — perched on a bacteriological powder keg. Meritchell draws me out of my sad philosophy. The girl comes by rubbing her eyes and asking me what time it is; her watch has stopped as well. Then Pep Junior appears with a zombie-like air. What a night he must have had between such red-hot beauties. He looks at them the out of the corner of his eye; they, however, are fresh and rested.

"Well, people," Captain Mendez tells us. "It is time to get moving. We are all going to help distribute the lorries with the weapons that should be heading to the checkpoint right now." He looks at me and my mouth opens to tell him that I came to be an "observer", tourist-style. Nevertheless, due to my curious nature, I do not open my mouth and I go with them. We are behind Jordi, the one from La Caixa trying to teach Catalan to an exuberant and luscious Peruvian woman with an ass that she moves so much like a cocktail shaker that it looks like it is about ready to explode. The Catalan is moving quickly with Ambar, which is the girl's name.

"You are very quiet, babydoll", says Pep, who always uses this adjective and other cute terms when he talks to me. Actually, I am engaging my intellect by trying to observe whether Meritchell or Jordi — or perhaps the apparently harmless Pep — are in the know, so to speak. I try to identify a signal between them, but found nothing for the moment. These people must be very prudent types. The truth is I have gone and twisted things up to the point that I suspect everyone. So, in order to not keep thinking in circles, I continue to stay close to Pep, who has just made a misstep and nearly pulled everyone down with him. A lot of Holsec indians are coming with us. The captain gives them food and they act as guides, since they know the mountain perfectly.

Looks like we are in Ozatlán and are headed to

the area around Quijilisco. The air already smells of the sea, for Quijilisco is located near the Pacific. The landscape is a plant fertiliser producer's dream, as we are surrounded by all kinds of colossal vegetation, enormous and immensely exuberant. The airplane sits on a plateau that we reach after leaving behind a narrow track with marks from the tyres of a truck.

When we get to point X, I confirm that the lorries are jeeps. There are six and they are painted green and have small curtains of the same colour. The entire team is working hard because I see (a number of planes must have come) that they are full of large wooden crates containing weapons manufactured in Spain, as I realise later. I consider the idea of opening up to Pep and telling him everything because I think the poor guy has his head in the clouds, that he has no idea of what is actually going on. My feet hurt from walking so much. To distract myself, I want to take a picture of the group as a memento of the holiday. But when I get ready to take it, Alain — with a broad grin — tells me not to. "It is best left for another day, is it not, my little island bird?" I would rather not argue about his reasons and put my camera away without a word. I tell Pep that I am tired and retrace my path, like in the story of Tom Thumb, to pay a visit to Giorgio's tent.

I do not make a big deal of it — unusual for me — and I do not invest much time in reaching it, checking to make sure that no one was following me on my way back. The tents are all similar and I am curious but scatter-brained, which why I took some time in finding the one with a Gucci brand sleeping bag, from Milan, with the initials G.M.M. My particular deduction leads me to conclude that is Giorgio Mario Marotti's tent. I go in; it is dark and smells strange. I am not carrying the little torch that has been so useful to me, so I wait for my eyes to adjust to the light. Nervous, I take a few breaths, trying to buy time. When I can see a little better, I open his sleeping bag carefully and the zip gets stuck. "Oh, I cannot do anything right!" At the bottom is a box of condoms from a well-known American brand. I put my hand back in. Damn, I hope it does not contain a snake guarding the secret. Afraid, I tell myself: "Relax, this stuff only happens in Spielberg films". The fact is that I have seen too many films, so I continue to put my hand deeper into the sleeping bag until I feel another hard package — but obviously not the kind I like. I turn it over carefully with my hand sweaty from the tension. What is more, my broken watch means that I cannot tell how long ago I left the group. They may be back, or on the way. I pull the package out with my hand. It is the case that Mr Sigal, the German, gave to Giorgio this morning. Without hesitating, I reacted quickly and take it to my tent. "Eva?" It is Meritchell's voice calling me. "I am on my way, dear" (the heat and the excitement have made me feel affectionate towards everyone). I hide the box containing the chemical weapons and go to talk with Meritchell — who is sweating like a sinner in church — accompanied by some native women making the food. "Eva, where have you been? Whenever there is work to do, you either hide or go to the toilet."

Afterwards, she lowers her voice and says to me, "That Italian guy, Giorgio, is very strange. He was going back and forth all night long. I do not know; I think that he is weird. And yesterday I thought I saw him talking in German via a small radio. When I saw him, he hid right away". "I do not know, girl", I answered her, very much in my role as a woman of the world, but I also think he is a bit strange". We fall silent because the others are arriving and they are hungry. I drink Evian water from a big jug that Jordi brought. At the end of the meal when we are drinking some yerba mate, Pep Junior tells us the news: Amparo Soria has been murdered. She is lying behind a rock, the one where, just yesterday, I bathed myself in moonlight. Giorgio found her. She looked like she was asleep, except that she has a knife — like the ones the Indians carry to create a path in the jungle — brutally stuck in her abdomen. "She will not be doing any more shows at the Bagdad". That is obvious! The pallor of death, slowly and surely spreads over her face and, especially, over all her body, which is gradually showing signs of rigor mortis. Together, we all tried to get her out of there; her weight is surprising, the poor thing. There is no red tape to deal with in this part of the world. So, after putting her into a kind of sailor's duffel, but longer, that Mendez brought us, we proceeded to bury her in a spot not too far from the camp.

Pep Junior is definitely the one who gives us the latest camp news, because when we get back — exhausted, beat and rather worried — he tells us that Giorgio has disappeared with all the documents and his belongings and those of the unfortunate Amparo Soria.

With all this, it is now quite late and night falls on the camp before the main station can be informed via radio. Mendez gives me a sexy look and I comb my natural curls. I am starving and tell Pep. He brings me a bar of dark chocolate; he knows it is the kind I like best. He has understood that the way to a woman's heart is through her stomach and he wants to "encourage" me with a view to the rapidly approaching night, but he also knows very well that I am very picky when it comes to "fancyschmancy" moral hygiene; however, as things are going, the matter of the bed during this holiday is not going well, not well at all.

To a greater or lesser extent, everyone is smoking their joints — that is, coke — except me. In terms of diet, I take very good care of myself. So I am as healthy as they come and I keep myself in line. I return to the tent angry; the way I am feeling, and unable to screw Pep. I thought about the girl from Bilbao and cursed her mother. I get ready to get into my sleeping bag naked, because it is very hot. When I am showering and drying off, Pep shows up in a tender and romantic — in other words, sexy — mood.

"Baby, my girl with a china doll face: you really are not going to leave me with bread and water tonight, are you?" He caresses my chest lovingly and, when he is about to move to my left breast — before I get caught up, for I am not made of stone —I give him a good elbow in the ribs, protecting my health. Pep

slinks away, defeated. I am immersed in my sleeping
bag mulling over the day's events when I hear someone
slipping through the curtains and the zip of my tent. I
thought it would Pep, trying to make up, and look: I
see Captain Mendez' blue-black beard in the moonlight.
"Could we talk a little, gorgeous?" "Of course, Captain",
I responded, pulling my sleeping bag up to my chin,
fully engaged in my role in some film whose name I
cannot recall at the moment. Mendez tells me of his
ideals and his loneliness. He has a wife and five children
in Bogotá. Chatting, he is seated on my sleeping bag,
when I see a hideous snake slithering to my right. I was
going to scream, terrified, but Mendez quickly took
care of it with his guerrilla's sword. How long, wide and
thick it was! I am truly impressed and systematically
embrace the captain. His beard tickles me and I laugh.
"Hey, be quiet, girl. We are going to wake up the whole
camp and your husband will come. I have just sent him
a kilometre from here for guard duty." That is fine. I
kiss him and am feeling ready. I help him to get out of

his clothes (with so much on, he is nothing like me). I am finally able to see him in all his glory. It must be said that Mendez is hairy. I look for his dick, which I do not find because it is so small. However, it is nice and straight — the truth must be told — and quite feisty and guerrilla-like. Just in case, I put him inside me and we make delicious love, for I am almost hungrier than he is. Now it has been in-and-out, in-and-out, five times. Now I feel good. I am finally about to fall asleep when a timid hand opens the zip to my tent again. "Can I come in or were you sleeping?" The smiling face of Pep Junior appears. "Eva, do you mind if I come in?" "No, come in." I sit on my sleeping bag and wrap myself in my spare t-shirt. Since I am already awake, I take a small bottle of nail polish out of the backpack and start to touch up my nails. Pep Junior is devastated, grieving, heartbroken. "And Meritchell?" "She is with Jordi; they are having a big party in his sleeping bag." "But what about last night? Is it not going well?" "Last night, absolutely nothing, because and then..." "With the stuff going on in the jeep, it looked like there was going to be a second, less frustrating, part." Filled with compassion, I look at the poor guy. He seems about to start crying at any moment. "Listen, Eva, I am a virgin and when the time comes, it is hard for me to go for it." He looks at me with love and tenderness. Without me realising it, he caresses my nipples and, unintentionally, already wet I start to carefully open his zip, because he is very hard and I am afraid I will catch and hurt him. When I take it out, it is huge, and I carefully start to suck it gently, so that he does not come right away. But Pep holds on and takes the natural route. So then we both ride towards the sun and towards the violet moon and take the stars into our hands, feeling a new world created by our pleasure and for us alone. We fall asleep exhausted in each other's arms. At dawn, I feel thirsty. Pep is breathing calmly near me, hugging me half asleep. I take one hand and pull it out; the tent door is half open and I continue to wake him up. He complains at first, then he laughs and, laughing and playing, we go to the waterfall. I help him to undress. "Come on, lazybones; come and get wet." I also undress quickly and we both start drinking the tepid water falling from the mountain. As we drink, we bite our lips hard, like two animal cubs. The moon, not yet set, lights us with a silvery halo. We head over to the grass and make savage love.

When we return to the tent, daylight appears over the hill and it is lovely to watch it together. Suddenly, I realise that someone has been snooping around inside my sleeping bag. Fortunately, I took the precaution of putting the box in my Pep Senior's sleeping bag which — standing guard — he was not going to use. I feel calm. The night has been rich in emotions and I slept like a rock entirely in the buff.

The sound of voices is what wakes me; it sounded like someone was arguing. I get dressed and run into Captain Mendez. He throws me a look of gratitude, which I return mechanically. He is with a man of colour dressed in military getup speaking to him quietly. I try to listen and it seemed they talking about Giorgio, who had disappeared.

Pep Junior brings me a banana while murmuring pleasantries in my ear. "Oh, how you are tickling me, Pep!"

Around noon, the other Pep turns up and the captain summons us. He is extremely busy today. "A certain Giorgio Marotti is a man who has been specially prepared by the AARC (Anti-American Anti-Communist Revolutionary Corps). Despite his "good-guy" face, Interpol and the KGB and searching frantically for him. That is one of his many disguises; he is highly dangerous. We have been on his trail for some time, but he has always managed to get away, vanishing like smoke." We discussed the delicate mission that, without a doubt, brought us here. I also realise that he has just had a private little chat with Pep. Giving Pep Junior a reassuring look, I drag his father behind some bushes. I tell him everything, without leaving out the detail of the snake, which some of the native women took out of my tent. But it looks like today is the day of the fresh new, since Captain Mendez (the guy never stops; I had not finished talking with Pep) summons us to tell us that we have all been expecting for some time to hear: Amparo Soria was a dyed-in-the-wool AARC activist: an international spy between East and West. The noise of a motor cut him off; as excited as we were by these important events, we had not heard the late-model helicopter land near us in a hurricane of wind, forcing me to grab tightly on to the two Peps. The door opens and what do my eyes see? "It is nothing more or less than the uber-famous, unbeatable, incredibly beautiful, Baroness of Fifi Pan Pan. Hallelujah!" At last I get to see her in person. Me, a devotee of cheap romantic tabloids, although — since I do not often go to the hairdresser — I read them where no one can see me. She is a fixture at all the jet set's parties. She always lights them up with her eternally naturally perfect smile, lending them that touch of distinction. How wonderful and how she subjugates the plebs! She stands out among the men! She is synonym of women's jealousy! She is one word: IT IS SHE. My plebeian nature could not prevent my crotch from sweating when I saw her in person. A person of nobility, and of greatness, where all the graces came together in an excess of the Creator's zeal, and my mouth begins to... "Ohhh!, but where have I seen that face? Because it is not just that I know it from the tabloids", I muse to myself, "but, see how we find this gorgeeooouus woman with her long locks fluttering in the wind". Mendez introduces me to her. She offers an outstretched hand that I — affected by tabloiditis — am... about to kiss? "Did Mendez want to have a ménage à trois tonight in the tent?"

While the idea turns me on — and to relax a bit after so much excitement — I go with the two Peps to inspect the area. The days are passing quickly and we should do a little sightseeing in some of these frankly gorgeous places. Back at the camp, we find the Baroness of Fifi Pan Pan comfortably installed in her Christian Dior model tent, along the entire group, who are waiting for dinnertime. With her usual charm, the Baroness of Fifi Pan Pan shares all the latest gossip with us. I am dying to ask her about her oft-photographed kids, but the lady will not let me get a word in edgewise. I finally decide to eat my corncake while I mull over these questions: What is such a renowned personality doing in these parts? And who does her teeth remind me of? Pep Junior continues working on me fervently and that is what I like. And if he keeps on like this, I will not be able to finish eating and his father is not on guard duty tonight. In other words, we will have to see how we can work it out, and never better said.

As always, Captain Mendez will — unintentionally — come to my aid. Finishing dinner, Pep Junior's father reminds him that he is supposed to be on guard duty today, and that clarifies my night. Today, I will sleep. Then, after listening to the group and their magnificent guitars, I will disappear into the tent with Pep, tired from not having slept the previous night, almost like me, but for different reasons. We fall asleep like babies in our own sleeping bags. At midnight, some voices and noises wake me up and I go outside to see what is going on. Around the fire are Captain Mendez, the Baroness of Fifi Pan Pan, Jordi, Merichell and a small group of others, a chronicler of the jet set would say. They continue to eat. The Baroness had quite an appetite! With her savoir faire, she adroitly avoids the eructions that inevitably reach her from the nearby Mendez, whose breath most certainly did not smell of sponge cake. The Baroness, dressed very simply tonight, is adorned with a silver-and-cord neckless — a gift from one of her ex-husbands — which will surely be all the rage this season in the fashion media. Meritchell feels melancholy tonight and begins to spew it all on me. It appears that this girl is involved in Barcelona with a married man, one of those who like to turn on other men's ovens as well as their own, but never deciding between one and the other. They never leave their own while continuing to turn on those of others. As I am rather familiar with the type, I tell her not to be stupid. Since she has no kids, she should look for something better. Without realising it, we ended up alone, talking. She goes after Jordi and I go to my tent. I open the zip, and a hand grabs my throat roughly. I am going to scream, but I already feel the cold blade of a knife against my left rib, which convinces me to keep silent. "Come on, gorgeous, where did you stash the box?" I shudder. I know the voice, but my panic prevents me from thinking. "I know nothing of the box you are talking about", I answer in my usual sweet voice, playing stupid, something I do very well.

Afterwards, it all happened so quickly. With one karate chop, Pep throws the aggressor's knife to the floor, where the two are struggling. They do not let me take part in the fight, although the truth is that I tried to. I quickly drew the gun I always carry hidden in my panties next to my ass and aimed at them. But... it is Giorgio! The Baroness of Fifi Pan Pan is Giorgio? The surprise leaves me so stunned that I react wrong, while Pep is gently nibbling my neck; he how knows how much I love that, the sly devil. I whack the Baroness in the head with a high heel shoe I always carry stashed in my backpack, just in case. He drops to the floor like a sack of flour. Between Pep and I, we quickly search him and realise that the Baroness has a penis like a Stone Age menhir. It was Giorgio in one of his many disguises. He had adopted this one to watch the jet set. Pep has the box that Giorgio had come for well hidden, but how to make it disappear? Deadly as is, it would be better to give or send it to... which government? This lady had another surprise waiting for us hidden under her exquisite and very pure wool skirt: a letter. It contained just a few words written in German. Since I have taken a Bavarian cooking class in Heidelberg, I understand the language perfectly and this allowed me to translate it quickly. The author of the letter writes a few short lines to a Mr Sigal whom, I assume, lives in Berlin, works at the Pabis laboratories and must meet Giorgio in Windsor, England to give him new supplies at a visit to the castle the following Sunday with the first group of tourists. He will carry a red-and-white striped umbrella so he can be recognised. We give the Baroness — excuse me — Giorgio a shake, but he is already stiffer than a board. "Good heavens, I have killed him! So many karate classes to stay in shape and then they say that it is useless anyway; tell me about it. Well, as dead as he is, he is another one who will not be doing any more spying. "I am so hot today, that I would not even be able to locate Mendez's thing; it is so small." I take the low road; I just love to philosophise; it relaxes me at certain moments of great tension. And the little red light went on. "I will go to Windsor! But what day is it?" In this high-up place on top of the world, I have forgotten what day it is. "It is Saturday morning! Then, with the difference in time zones. How quickly; I have to really hurry." Quickly, Pep, the captain and I ready the plan.

While Pep and Mendez finalise the details, I put on my headphones with the cassette of Dire Straits that gets me all lovely-dovey, and that is the state Pep Junior finds me in when he finishes standing guard. We kiss tenderly. The memory of the last hours of love shared between us beats in us and makes us quiver. We laugh and kiss, happy to be alive. The jungle that surrounds is a worthy frame for our passion. It is like getting onto a carnival merry-go-round full of colours. But we had to come back down to earth. We met up with his father and the captain, that some further steps. It is decided; I will go alone to Windsor Castle. I needed to take the flight out to London this afternoon, but from Mexico; it is clear that we must hurry. Obviously, we had to move fast. Both Peps, Meritchell and Jordi will also travel with me. We are going to bring them up to date in their tent, where they are curled up together inside their sleeping bag. We explain everything to them because they did not understand anything and were aware of even less. The moment to say our goodbyes — always so sad — comes. We have to say goodbye to entire camp and get into Mendez's jeep — the same one we came in — except, of course, Amparo and Giorgio. They have gone to their reward. A mixed-raced woman also rides with us. We reach the road back quickly. The captain knows it well and drives as if the jeep had a firecracker up its ass, very fast. The guy is a real tiger behind the wheel. It is a good thing there is no one ahead of is and the only thing he has to dodge is trees. In order to avoid getting sick, I hold on to both Peps; foresighted, I breathe deeply the air along the road and fall asleep.

Once the car stops, I wake up mechanically. We are about to leave El Salvador. Alain, with another jeep, is next to a macuy tree, a long-lived species very common in these parts. I got the impression that a furtive tear was shining in the captain's eye. I also have a knot tightening in my stomach and manage to get rid of it quickly. He gives me a little gun as a memento and leaves with his luscious dark-skinned lady. She is quite attractive and surely, on the way back, she will apply herself to making him forget. This is what I was thinking while Alain's jeep was racing through Ahuachapán's virgin jungle. From the trees, some marmosets, or monkeys, observed us with — I imagine — tiny surprised eyes. We are racing towards Mazatenango at what seems to be an exaggeratedly fast, almost supersonic, speed. The fact is that Alain drives like a madman, just like the captain. He surely would not get a driving licence like this in Montpellier.

Pep Senior and Alain have joined the club of Cohiba smokers. I have always said that there are some things that one gets used to quickly. We know this very well in Spain and they lick their cigars a lot; it looks like they are going to swallow them. Pep Junior is sitting behind with Jordi and me and he gives me a good telling off that is much healthier than tobacco. The forest, or virgin jungle, passes quickly. We leave behind the small monkeys; now we are passing through a small valley with very poor shacks scattered here and there. Chiquimulilla, Tacahá Valley, and now we are headed towards the city of Cuauhtamoc, as Alain tells us between drags on his Cohiba. And the sea breeze penetrates our nostrils with that smell of Pacific seaweed and sharks. Before leaving the camp — and to generate some luck in the hope that it would be good luck — I put on a new pair of really cute tiny red lace panties with little bows, because with so many tortillas and beans I just might split them. Another jeep awaits us in Salinas de la Cruz. It has been updated by the captain, who has all the details. We bid Alain good-bye with misty hearts. And, here we are, passing through border checkpoints and leaving behind this beautiful part of South America, on the way to Great Britain.

My plane leaves before the one to Barcelona, so I go through passport control and say good-bye at once. "In war, I squeeze all my feelings dry", Napoleon once said before a battle, and I head towards the tunnel leading me to my plane without turning around even once. Pep, always cautious, has hidden the box well and has just entrusted me with it discreetly in a plastic bag with the name of a department store. I carry it in my left hand, holding it carefully. When I get on the plane, I look back and see the two Peps and the little group waving me good-bye from a big terrace in the Mexican airport. They're like little heads of pins waving little canes; the new continent bids me good-bye.

I find my seat on the plane next to a nice attractive man of colour. In the seats behind me are two American yuppies of the kind omnipresent on airplanes. Near him is a very interested woman. She is constantly caressing him, telling him how excited she is about getting to know London. She looks at him with tenderness thinking, perhaps, about the boutiques she is going to visit in England, and he looks at her thinking, also perhaps, about the times they will make love. Besides, his company is paying for the whole trip, and his nights are going to be entertaining. Poor woman. Although seeing her smile, I imagine that she will never figure out how she is being manipulated and, like Victor Hugo said before he began writing *Les Miserables*: "he who does not realise, does not suffer". Tired of cheap philosophy, I pass the time looking out the window and fall asleep. I dream about Captain Mendez, who comes towards me wearing traditional embroidered skirts. He lifts up the various layers he is wearing and calls me, his dick standing straighter than ever. Or stiffer than ever. "Is something wrong?" the dark-skinned man next to me enquires politely. "You were talking in your sleep about a dick. How are you?" He says this to me in English. I deduce that he does not understand Spanish. It is the altitude or recent emotions. What actually happened to me is that, suddenly, uninhibited, I grab his, I open his fly and give him one of those "first peace and then glory" blowjobs. The guy is in heaven and so am I, since cum gets me going, raises my blood pressure, deactivates my nerve impulses and sends me quickly into orbit. Afterwards, we talk for a while; what a shame, the guy is going to Bristol; he is not staying in London. "Do not miss the opportunity, Eva; it is just two days", I advise myself and continue on, while the passengers put on their masks to sleep. The man from Atlanta has not the slightest doubt about progress in terms of racial discrimination, and also, as Pep would say, "Baby, you do not leave me a single drop as proof", and that is just how I am; a perfectionist through and through.

When finished, I smooth my curls and go to the bathroom like any good girl would. Afterwards, I go back down the aisle thinking about face on the agent in service to her British Majesty. Pep — who is involved in everything — took the trouble to notify him, and he is waiting for me at Heathrow. How will I recognise him? My spirit was tormented by this doubt and, since there is only one thing I like more than getting it from the front — getting it from behind — that is what I do with Roberto — as the man from Atlanta is called — scandalising a passenger heading to the toilet who surprised us behind the little curtain of the aisleway in full ecstasy. I do not even know how, but we manage to get back to our seats and sleep like babies. We are awakened by the voice of the stewardess offering us coffee. I ask her how long before we land and she says just a few minutes. The yuppie asshole continues to explain things to his partner and, since there is nothing that bores me more than a yuppie asshole, I try to not listen to his monotonous and placid voice. I sit down and enclose myself in the deepest part of myself and of the cloud-filled scenery I see through the window. We are landing and it is extremely nice. We land quickly and, with my little baggage, I have no problems at Customs. I bid Roberto a pleasant good-bye and we exchange business cards. I take the stairway that leads me to the main lobby with my senses on full alert, but see no trace of Her British Majesty's agent, 009 with a licence, I think. I began to feel like something was not right and my heart was pounding wildly. I have the letter that was under Giorgio the Baroness Fifi Pan Pan's skirt. It is stuck sweatily between my butt and the red panties that I think are not going to bring me any luck today.

I head over to the toilet, wash myself and also put on a very, very cute little leopard thong very appropriate for the day and on to the attack! The purse with the weapons on my right, I leave the toilet ready to take on the world. I start by chugging a double espresso sitting at the counter of the bar and some raisin cake, which is one thing I love about England. I still have not had my period, and this worries me, almost as much as the deadly weapons I am carrying. "Jeez, what a chest! How fat I have become." This gives me thought and I think it is likely not from being touched. "Relax, little one", talking myself into getting a grip. "You will see how everything soon works out." A little boy, who has been annoying me for quite a while, keeps on hitting my foot as I am sitting on a bar stool. The kid extends his hairy hand and puts a letter under my cup of coffee, while a cavernous voice comes out of his tiny body: "Did you fall out of the tree, stupid?" HER BRITISH MAJESTY'S AGENT IS... A DWARF!

While I recover from my surprise, he assures me that he is 009, not 007, who has had a lot of facelifts and has ended up this small. 007 is in a rest home for the elderly in Worthing, and he ended up in the first row. "What kind of staff they must have in Scotland Yard", I reflect, while he accompanies me to the car park, where he has left an old Austin and we quickly get on the road to Windsor. It is Sunday and there may be a traffic jam. "I hope I will have time tomorrow for a walk around Oxford Street", I think, while the car passes through the English countryside, which is always very beautiful and so well maintained. This does not surprise me at all, since England is ruled by a woman. Clothing is not too expensive, of modern quality and the buttons do not fall off; in other words, they are well sewn. "By the way, are you carrying weapons?" "Yes, my orders are for you to give them to me." "Well, with how much I want to get rid of the little bag in question, when you stop, I will give them to you, 009. And what are you going to do with them?" "Our teams will make sure they disappear without any danger to humanity. Listen, what numbers have you got, gorgeous?" the dwarf asks me gallantly. "Oh, they still have not given me any number", I answer humbly. I quickly bring George — that is the agent's name — up to date: the deaths of Amparo Soria and of Baroness of Fifi Pan Pan (Giorgio) and everything else. After making me talk, this SOB — the dwarf — knew everything, or almost everything, because he had spoken by phone with Pep. This time, the parties have joined together to beat this crazy Nazi who, with help from the AARC (Anti-American Anti-Communist Revolutionary Corps) terrorist group, this group of savages have made two formerly enemy parties join together to fight against them. I tell him, as humbly as I can, about my part of my mission preventing the Baroness/Giorgio from contaminating the waters with the AIDS virus. The car slows down at the entrance to Windsor Castle. The other cars are queuing in front of us. George has told me about the plan of action. We park next to the entrance to the car park and head, with several hundred other tourists, towards the castle. It is a splendidly bright day and the sky is a bright clear blue that brings a special sharpness to the surroundings. We are visiting the castle when a tourist goes to take a photo near the well while the dwarf has gone to the toilet; it must be a Finn, for he is so blond he is almost albino. I react quickly, stepping aside when the camera revolver begins to fire. I push aside a herd of Japanese tourists who bump into each other with their cameras, and pull the little pistol Mendez gave me from my panties. Behind a battlement. I see him. Without a second though, I pull the trigger and he falls writhing to the ground, dying immediately. Behind me, George's voice. He still has the smoking gun in his hand. We have had the assistance of Her Majesty's agent. We lack the time to admire our fine shooting, for I have just seen Sigal who — having witnessed the death of his agent — racing away across another battlement. The agent and his apprentice agent — I — split up and quickly head over to surround him. I climb cautiously, step by step, but uh-oh! I feel something very cold on the nape of my neck and it gives me the shivers: it is the barrel of a Magnum 412. "My little friend, you have not stopped annoying me." I recognize that anal-retentive voice. "Herr Professor Sigal!" I try not to shake. When

I feel the gun fire, I bid a quick and emotional good-bye to my loved ones (who will take care of Leyla from now on?). Nobody is indispensable and my time has come... Suddenly, I hear a bullet behind me. "I am alive!" I turn around and see Herr Professor lying on the ground looking exactly like an Egyptian mummy. He is surrounded by George's agent colleagues, who killed him.

After I reached the hotel and showered, Pep rang me from Barcelona. Tomorrow we are going to the doctor so he can get treated for the little blennorrhagica problem, he promises me, congratulating me on the outcome of the operation. "You seem worried, little one. Is there something that is not right?" I reassure him and go to bed. My period still has not come. When I got back to the hotel I bought one of those instant pregnancy tests at the chemists and it turned out positive. A friend of mine who is a Vidal Sassoon hairdresser gave me the address and they are expecting me tomorrow at the clinic.

I am trying to not think about anything. My friend lent me the pounds sterling; she is unable to come with me because she has a lot of work. In Spain, I would have had a lot of problems. I would have got everything ready and fallen in love with that little thing that I know is inside me and that I am not going to bring to this crazy, on-edge world. It would be another candidate for unemployment or spectator of the injustices of people contradicting one another of those who manipulate, guided by their own interests, in their favour, corruption, and so on.

And that is why I am now calm when they prepare me, and that is also why I close my eyes and enter placidly into a pink cloud when the nurse takes me in the stretcher and opens the doors to the surgery...

THE END

Barcelona 1986

AMANDINA IS UNDER A STAR

"If I do not tell him, you die and truly leave here wealth and strength. If it is not as I say, may this migdala take me to my grave, to the house of the dead."

(African *migdala* by an unknown author)

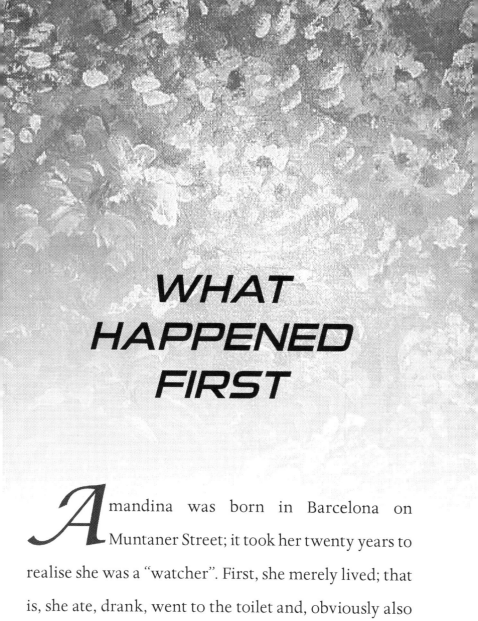

WHAT HAPPENED FIRST

*A*mandina was born in Barcelona on Muntaner Street; it took her twenty years to realise she was a "watcher". First, she merely lived; that is, she ate, drank, went to the toilet and, obviously also washed. Thirty years later, one morning Amandina was amazed to discover for herself the power of her gaze. She observed things, people, cars or clouds. Amandina was an exceptionally fortunate "watcher" of the great cinema around her. It is not that nothing ever had ever happened to her, no. Her parents died in a tragic accident; the gas tap in the kitchen opened by accident and they did not wake up that long-ago morning.

By then, Amandina was already married and had four children, a boy and a girl, and a set of twins. One day, her husband did not come home. Amandina waited for him until dinnertime, but finally had to clear the table. She did not even taste the soup. She went directly to the bathroom and flushed it down the toilet. Afterwards, she ate a crust of bread and a piece of Manchego cheese, along with one of those yellow, tart apples called Golden in the market.

She did not have time to worry or to call the police, since at midnight the phone range, nearly waking the children. Amandina, who was falling asleep, picked up: it was her husband saying he was never coming back.

Then came the divorce with all that mess of

lawyers and masses of paperwork, interminable boring meetings, and family talks. Finally, the final verdict.

Amandina kept the children with all the usual conditions and so on. Amandina took them to the park and fed them, managing the best she could or knew how, and so a decade passed, apparently without problems. At least if there were any, Amandina was not aware of them. First, one child left, then another, and then another. Amandina tried to hold on to them, but when she saw they were happier that way, so was she. Things were changing in the city. In Amandina's opinion, the noise was becoming excruciatingly obvious. So many cars, so much honking, braking, skidding and more honking. The noises dug into her frontal lobes and pursued her head like a streamer carried forward by the wind at first, and then towards the back and she was never able to avoid it, never able to escape from the noise.

How boring; it was so uncomfortable to not be able to communicate. And she thought no more. She had so many things to watch, was so greedy to check on, feel the strange buzz of the flies, the peal of the bells, the road of the airplanes. She found refuge with a folding bed in the ironing room, the only room in the house that opened on to the courtyard, and the noise sounded muffled, distant. Amandina had found her refuge, and when she left it, she thought about it, the refuge that awaited her. Just for her, for Amandina, so she could rest.

"I am a creature of city and I must act like one", and tried to observe the others attentively so she could copy them as skilfully as possible. She realised the futility of getting irritated and how ridiculous arguing over nothing was, and never did it again. She observed that people always seemed to be in a hurry, both coming and going, to get to the same place at the same time, like a carousel at the fair. Amandina walked at a steady pace, calmly, with measured breath, and learnt to listen. She listened and listened on the phone whenever the others called; she learnt the noise of the wood when it creaked, the sound of the bus when it braked, and the unexpectedly loud voice that dropped coming from the lady living in the left-hand apartment on the sixth floor, the dog barking downstairs at the same time and always in the same tone, and the noise of the lift and the rickety kitchen cabinet, and the silence of the night, its noise, of silence, which was like the trail of a silver star, like the Magi's, maybe, and Amanda smiled happily, but on the inside, with a smile in her gut, very authentic and genuine.

One day, Amandina met Socias Suliveda, who was the minister of state or something. He was married to a South American painter and immediately felt attracted by Amandina. The following week they made love. Amandina had learned to tighten and loosen the labia of her vagina over and over. Socias felt was enthralled with this movement which, in all his 54 years, had never heard of, and he did not want to let go of Amandina, at least for the moment. He opened a bank account in her name and also bought her a jewellery and gifts boutique in a shopping centre. So, Amandina could travel to India or Brazil and return with her baggage full of necklaces, bracelets and beads and selling them for three times their value in Barcelona and once a week meet up with Socias in that hotel in the upper part of the city, and open and close, close and open. Amandina was an expert. She could have been a professor, as her labia gripped Socias' penis so tightly that he came back more enthralled every night. Amandina watched him, especially afterwards, while he poured himself some whisky on the rocks and went to shower. She watched him. Socias and his front-and-back pot belly, big ass — strange on a man — and his triple chin, too. Amandina checked him out calmly and slowly, wrapped in the linen sheet. She was nearly asleep when he turned over to kiss her before falling asleep. That evening he had told his wife that he was in Amsterdam. Amandina wondered vaguely if she had bought the story, but she truly did not care. And so a year passed, and another...

She took a taxi and all this, right in the middle of the

crazy traffic. Amandina saw metal monsters, felt her nose filling with the sharp smell of nerves and repression like a grey cloud with a touch of violet, unworried in the middle of the long road that continued to Las Ramblas that the taxi driver — increasingly irritated with the other drivers or metal monsters — usually took. And so, limping along, Amandina finally made it down Las Ramblas de las Flores. She finally had the impression that she always took the same taxi driver, although he always drove different cars, and that she always ran into the same pedestrians, although it was at different times on different days. Only the sky was changed colour; the sky and the temperature, too. Everything else — everything — was wrapped in a truly stupid monotony. "I must be the stupid one", she thought. "Well, I will try to observe better", so she sharpened her sight, her hearing and her sense of smell. Even in bed she concentrated, opening and closing her labia with real skill; later, she slept peacefully and almost happily.

Time passed and her daughter, the only child of the

four still with her, was about to turn thirteen; she was tall, beautiful, intelligent and cheerful. "This is much better", thought Amandina, watching how she grew and was transforming daily into a beautiful woman. Amandina had a large home, and one day she realised that the many things she had inside were more than were necessary. Home from school, Maria found the house empty; her mother had sold it all to the antiques dealer. Some large lorries had come and filled their empty bellies with little Louis XV sofas, chairs, marble and inlaid wood consoles, Napoleonic mirrors and many, many more things. Amandina danced a jig in the empty white room; this was so much better. Maria, who was no fool, said she was right; she loved her mum, and she went to her room to study. What was left she took care to burn later in the big fireplace in the lounge: the books, the paintings, everything the antiques dealer had not wanted. Absolutely everything except Maria's room of black and metallic furniture. It belonged to her daughter, and Amandina respected others' property.

She had seen this in people who acted properly. She also left her folding bed in the maid's room, along with a short ladder like a stool that served as a bedside table. Amandina felt much more liberated, as if she had no, or much less, ballast.

The big TV, Maria's hi-fi set and the Spanish guitar that Amandina only played when she felt like it. One Saturday afternoon, Amandina ran into Socias Suliveda and his wife the South American painter at a concert at the Palau. Amandina was with Maria, and they were heading during the intermission to the bar when they saw each other. Socias made the introductions. "Your friend looks like someone has cheated on her," Socias' painter wife said to him. "You mean cheated on you", he thought while he paid for the refreshments and helped his wife put on her mink coat.

Sometimes, Amandina thought she had too many paintings. Then it did not matter to her whether it was three in the morning or four; with large scissors she would go snip-snip to the canvasses and the wood and tried to make use of them by building a fire in the fireplace. The next day, armed with newspapers and alcohol-soaked cotton wool, the empty wooden frames would appear with the ripped canvass. Amandina was calmly trying to make a torch with matches, with the newspaper lit and then put it on the wood. Futile, the house quickly filled with smoke and even the neighbours were alarmed, for they had seen and smelled the smoke and the odour which escaped from under the front door.

Maria came home from school and, with a look of tenderness and maturity, picked up the balls of grey formed by the burnt newspaper, which crumbled into ash at her touch, and the singed but intact wood of the pictures. Amandina looked at her with eyes full of excuses, and so it was until the following winter. "I need to find an axe", Amandina would say to herself, but the forest was far from the city and from the hellish machines, where there was only asphalt, noise and nerves, and to get there she needed at least a horse.

Amandina was a very poor rider and, besides, she lacked a horse. "I will have to speak with Socias Suliveda", she thought. But he embraced her, sought out her labia, first sticking his finger there, then another, and another, and he tore off her clothing, so she knew what awaited her. He placed her on the bed and Amandina concentrated on repeating the exercise that Socias apparently liked so much. Afterwards, exhausted, she always forgot about the horse and did not remember it until Socias had gone.

Socias enjoyed shopping. He was a faultless shopper: he always came back holding a package. When it was big, Amandina would get frightened. "What could be inside!", she would think. She would have to open it, take it, fix the papers, take the trash bag out to the stairway, and so on.

He came back from one of his trips to Germany as a minister with his face lit up and a square package. Amandina thought: "Now, what is this?" Well, they were some engraved Bohemian crystal whisky glasses that Socias had picked out in Mannheim's best boutique. Amandina loved to pee in them.

One day, after they had been playing vaginal open and close, and Amandina felt like peeing. Socias went to the kitchen; he was thirsty and got up to get some water from the fridge. Amandina was there, crouched, meticulously trying to improve her accuracy. The fine pale yellow stream that fell from among her long, thick pubic hair landed with a small and aristocratic noise into Socias' favourite whisky glass. He felt surprised at not feeling angry. On the contrary; he felt a tenderness deep inside watching her, from behind, with her head tilted forward and checking her shot carefully. "You look like a little girl", he said. "I stopped being one years ago", she answered, finishing her long, very long and pleasant piss. The glass was full, ready to overflow. She picked it up carefully and poured it down the sink while she washed it. Afterwards, they went back to bed and fell into a deep and restful sleep.

Day by day, Socias felt increasingly pulled to

Amandina who, without leaving his side — quite the opposite — went every day to the same place he had found her. Not that she was feeding a feeling of adversity against Socias, not even reluctance, much less disgust. Not at all. She simply had no particular feeling at all. She shared his bed one day a week and that was it. And so passed a month, and another, and a year, and another one after that, and another was passing.

Amandina continued practising her exercises of observing life, trying to accommodate herself more and more to her environment. She copied the reactions, the attitudes she glimpsed out of the corner of her eye in the street, in the queue at the cinema or on the bus. However, she never managed to copy the gestures in their essence, for Amandina did not feel the motivations, passions, the core that drove those gestures. She was also well aware of being incapable of ever feeling them. It was clear, but she was indifferent to this as well. Life washed through Amandina, although her enormous, elephantine "watching" curiosity obstinately awaited the surprise of one day finding something new.

Amandina lived in a city of tall, grey, damp houses. Her position, leaning slightly outside and to the side, allowed her ample observation of the people, cars, gestures, hear the noise, barking, honking, that she had learnt to differentiate perfectly. Her obvious lack of a practical and critical sense of judgement put her in an even more advantageous situation for being swept away by her insatiable curiosity.

Amandina met Miguel at midday one summer crossing the road on her way home. Miguel was good-looking, about twenty or twenty-two years, tall and thin, with short, thick hair and green eyes. He spoke to Amandina, "Hey, do I know you from Ibiza or Aro Beach? Were you at Ku last year?" Amandina had never been on Ibiza, much less at Ku, but did not answer right away, as she was trying to figure out whether Miguel's eyes were blue or green, although she still did not know that Miguel's name was Miguel. There was a sudden gust of wind and Amandina could smell Miguel's underarms. It was summer and a smell sour and bitter grazed the nostrils and liked this. She decided to give him her phone number. Miguel called and called and Amandina already knew his name, age and also that he was in the second year of law school. He finally had his date with Amandina at six o'clock in the evening on a corner near her house. Miguel was waiting; he was nervous and burnt from Sitges' sun. He took her to a friend's house; he said the family was on holiday. They went into the flat, in the upper part of the city, bourgeois, large, wooden furniture— also bourgeois— covered with white sheets. The floor was wood, "Be quiet; take off your shoes. One of my mother's uncle lives upstairs and might hear us". Amandina smelled his breath. She entered a small room like a young woman, two narrow beds.

"Where do you want?"

"In that big one, your parents'", answered Amandina.

They went in. Oak bed, a print of a virgin over the

headboard. Amandina sat on the bed. Miguel motioned to her to not make any noise.

"Look, Miguel, you should have brought someone who is deaf and dumb!" Amandina liked to scream when she made love, she liked it. "Call me when I get back from Brazil, okay?" She left without having even kissed him, but this time making noise and out the front door.

WHAT HAPPENED AFTERWARDS

*A*mandina sat on the raffia seats on the boat's deck. It was ready to cast off. The June sky — the green June sky — that day, was navy blue and the firecrackers and rockets sparkled on the night's verbena. A foreign voice asked what the party was all about. "It's the verbena of Saint John." The voice belonged to a rather attractive burly Dutchman who was also headed to Palma de Mallorca like Amandina and Maria. Later, he began to tell her all about himself; he was charming. Amandina looked at Barcelona's sea with Montjuic and Tibidabo in the distance and at the gulls flying around them; she envied them. Maria came by, excited by the amazing discoveries she had made during her tour of the boat.

They gradually left the port behind and Barcelona grew smaller and smaller. Amandina was cold and headed off to the cabin. She fell asleep at once, like a satisfied baby. The next day, everything went quickly: a quick wash, a bite of breakfast and a dash to the deck to see the boat arrive at the island. The imposing cathedral so liked by George Sand a century before was silhouetted against the blue sky, the rocks, the water; they were truly unique.

Amandina and Maria went down to get into the car and disembark onto the port's docks.

The Dutchman completely slipped Amandina's mind; she did not recall not saying good-bye to him until night-time, while showering before getting into bed. Only one thing left Amandina perplexed: the vague impression she felt in certain moods and in certain subjects of one sex or the other that revealed defects that, in her eyes, were unforgivable, like jealousy, lack of sensitivity or obvious ignorance. She was surprised and frightened by people who stare openly, murmuring or openly showing obviously aggressive feelings of boredom or arrogance.

This irritated Amandina to the point that it had made her lose her cool. She was totally incapable of understanding envy and its derivatives, and the kinds of behaviour this triggers. Aggression — towards her or her daughter — would cause Amandina to seethe, as did decidedly self-righteous and false advice.

It would take her hours to recover, to find the calm; sometimes she would spend an entire sleepless night trying — fruitlessly — to understand it.

With obvious childlike naiveté, Amandina did not understand. Another Amandina should have been made in order for her to eventually understand certain human feelings, in part easily understandable, that are derived from these reactions. But not for Amandina, for it was impossible for someone who had never felt envy to understand what it can cause.

Amandina was incapable of loving someone badly, although if she sensed ill will towards her — she was very vulnerable — she felt very, very deeply hurt, like a wounded animal, an animal that does not understand why the hunter has hurled a spear into his back. That burns her, hurts her and surprises her, too. Amandina was not able, did not know how, to avoid it and she continued this way, completely undefiled with these humanly negative feelings.

Home from Mallorca, when she was taking the photos to be developed, Amandina met Amalia. She was in the queue in front of her, and she noticed that she had interesting boots; they were like cowboy boots from the far west and had studs on the toes and heels. Her blue jean jacket with a terry cloth Bugs Bunny on the back was also cool. She turned and then smiled at Amandina, and so began a friendship that would last quite some time. Amalia worked in a hostess club in the upper part of the city and was doing very well, judging by what she said.

Amandina was the leaf fallen from the tree of a wealthy family, with all the consequences — often numerous — this entails. Before, when she was a married lady, things were very different. Afterwards, there were no more phone calls, not for birthdays or even Maria's name day. There were no more invitations and even the neighbours on the fourth and seventh floors stopped saying hello to her. Everything was different. Not that this concerned Amandina too much; she simply was aware of the fact; she confirmed it and accepted it as something inherent in her current situation. Amandina tried to properly assess attitudes and things. A big joke, a wry grin that was worth living for, forever in her favour. And this was like exercise for her. Life was slipping through Amandina's fingers because she so wanted to live it. She lacked the hours, the minutes she needed to enjoy and feel life. Amandina had learned to live life fully and to try to enjoy every minute without wasting a breath. She got used to travelling alone. She enjoyed it; it allowed her to refine her practices of watching people, the world. When she had to travel, she arranged to do it an hour in advance. This way, she could watch and watch to her heart's content.

In the airport, past Customs, near the duty-free area, people's faces, their reactions, in the toilet, the particular noise made by the till in the boutique, the pages of the newspapers as they are turned, the sighs of exhaustion or nervousness of a man whose plane is delayed, the distant murmur of a batch of passengers who have just landed, the little boy playing with the toy car his mum has just bought to distract him from the toy stand, the old woman walking her dog before putting it in the wicket box, and those little noises that are so special that they are heard only in airports. And also that female voice offering information which you usually hear even in the toilet. What an exciting show for Amandina! Better than a good film.

From travelling so much, Amandina was able to perfectly distinguish every noise. She could have done it even with her eyes closed, one to one, with the particularity that each airport has its own, unique, noises. And also the looks from men and from certain women who, because of their appearance, a run-of-the-mill watcher would never have imagined, but which Amandina had. And she knew, she knew that you cannot take someone's measure based on appearance. On the contrary; people generally try especially to appear to be what they are not and will never be. They try to show feelings that are often not there, fake, and thus live and go through life on a never-ending collective wheel, with the consent and knowledge of all, and graciously accepted.

One late autumn afternoon, Amandina was on one of her frequent business trips to buy clothes for the Paris boutique when — lying on her bed in her room, dressed but shoeless — she saw a large office building through the window glass. It was early and there were people working. She felt observed and rose to close the curtains. Suddenly, she understood that she was also being observed by a clerk, perhaps, or that typist more or less like her. When Amandina was in bed at night with the door securely locked and the curtains tightly drawn, she felt like someone was watching her from on high, penetrating her privacy; someone very strong, enormous, pyramid-shaped. Something tore inside Amandina's stomach, it opened and a beam of light — until then been hidden in a thick fog — filled her with clarity and warmth. It was then that Amandina understood. It was then when she truly understood.

So, back in the city, when Socias Suliveda came to visit after Amandina had returned from one of her business trips to buy clothes, jewellery, things for the boutique, he found her distant, strange, as if lifeless... But what had they done to his Amandina? While they were in bed, Amandina let herself be used, but neither the lips above or the labia below made the contractions Socias loved so much. And her arms were like a doll's; loose and lifeless.

"Amandina, what is wrong, my dear?" Socias asked her, concerned.

"Nothing, except that you are a fat, old, greasy, oily, dirty-minded little runt," answered Amanda in a sure and extremely calm voice.

The words froze on Socias' tongue. He had stood up and his knees trembled while he looked at her with his eyes, somewhere between rage and stupor.

And that night it happened. It happened that Amandina began to rise and rise, floating. First, over the bed. The windows were opened by a gust of air and Amandina passed through them, rising and rising, climbing higher and higher until she reached the sky and landed on a silvery star. Amandina had finally found her star. Amandina was another in a harmonious universe that had welcomed her and given her peace and love forever.

THE END

Paris, 15 November 1987.

ABOUT THE AUTHOR

Born in 1942 in Barcelona to a Spanish father and US-born mother, as far back as she can remember Cristina Roldán has always considered herself a fighter for freedom in general and for women in particular. She always says that she leads by example, and that that's the best way to do it. She divided her time between Paris (where she studied) and Barcelona until the age of 46, when she and her daughter Sarah left behind city, home and everything familiar to never return to live there again. Although Cristina has written in French and Spanish since she was a small child, she finished this novel in 1986. She never wanted to publish it until now, and it is now being published for the first time. Cristina is also a painter and has worked as one, with exhibitions worldwide, including three times at Paris' Grand Palace with the Société des Artistes Français under the pseudonym Mariah Rodriguez (www. mariahrodriguez.net). Cristina is the mother of three children and grandmother of seven grandchildren and has lived in Paris, Brussels, Barcelona, Madrid and London.

Printed in the United States
By Bookmasters